Seeking an
AURORA

Blue Dot Kids Press
www.BlueDotKidsPress.com

Original North American edition published in 2020 by Blue Dot Kids Press, PO Box 2344, San Francisco, CA 94126. Blue Dot Kids Press is a trademark of Blue Dot Publications LLC.

Original New Zealand edition published by OneTree House Ltd.

This North American edition is published under exclusive license with OneTree House Ltd. Original North American edition edited by Summer Dawn Laurie and designed by Susan Szecsi.

Cataloging in Publication Data is available from the United States Library of Congress.
ISBN: 9781733121279

The illustrations in this book are hand-drawn
using soft pastels on Canson Mi-Teintes pastel paper.

Printed in China with soy inks

First Printing

Seeking an
AURORA

Written by Elizabeth Pulford
Illustrated by Anne Bannock

BLUE DOT KIDS PRESS

Late into the night

Dad nudged me awake.

"Come on," he said.

He pulled on my jacket,

woolly hat, and mittens.

"We're off to find an Aurora,"

he said.

"What's an Aurora?"

"Shush," said Dad
as we tiptoed past
Mom and my new
baby sister.

9

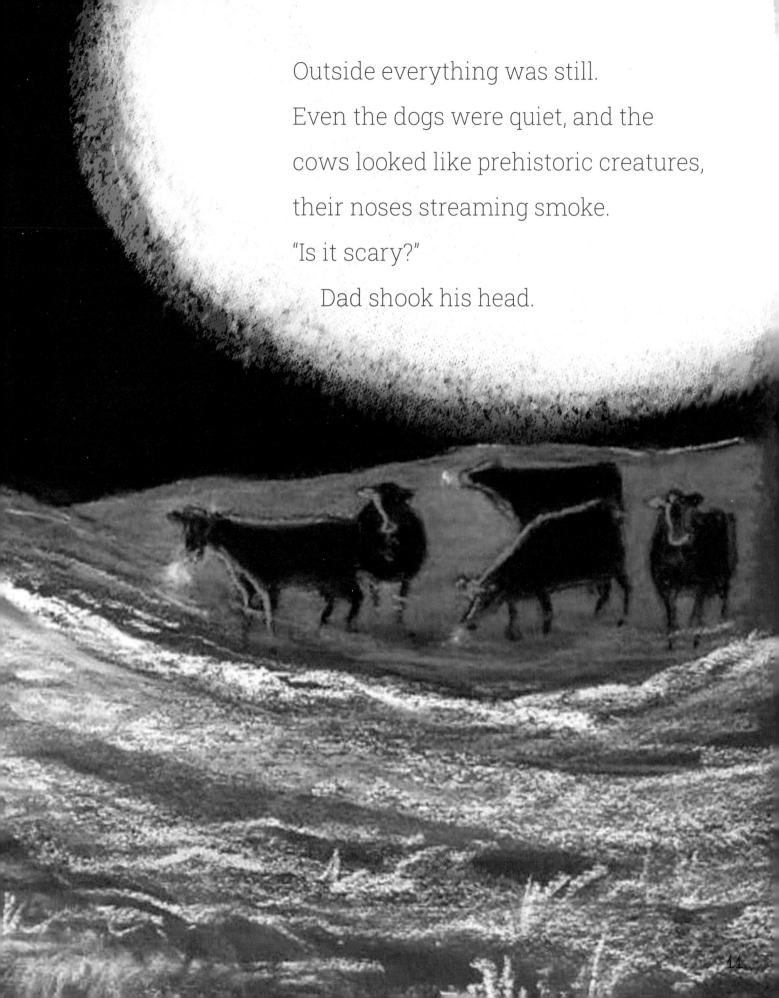

Outside everything was still.

Even the dogs were quiet, and the

cows looked like prehistoric creatures,

their noses streaming smoke.

"Is it scary?"

Dad shook his head.

As we trudged away,

I looked back at our house.

Back at the warm, buttery light

spilling from the kitchen window

and our footprints in the silvery frost.

As we climbed Bracken's Hill,

my breath huffed little ghosts,

while high above sailed the sky,

a ship of shivering stars.

"Dad, are stars in the Aurora?"

"No."

15

Up and up we climbed,

the moon glinting

between the trees

like a curved

splinter of glass.

"Is the moon

in the Aurora?"

"No," he said.

17

When we reached the top
of the steep hill,
we couldn't even see our house
or the dogs and cows.
Now we could see only the sky,
the stars, and the moon.

Dad sat on the stony ground,

with me real close to him.

"What's it like?"

"Look," he said . . .

My eyes popped

as wide wings of light

flew over the sky.

DANCING LIGHT, GLOWING AND...

COLORED RIBBONS SWIRLING AND TWIRLING,

GLIMMERING, SHIMMERING AND SHINING.

LIGHTING UP THE SKY ON THE STILL, DARK NIGHT.

25

Dad and I said nothing at all.

When we walked back home,

Dad talked and talked.

He told me everything he knew

about the Aurora.

"Amazing," I breathed,

back in the buttery kitchen,

and tucked at the table,

cozy in the sleepy silence.

"It was, wasn't it," said Dad.

Everything Dad Knew About the Aurora:

An aurora is a light display in the sky. A stunning natural spectacle when different rays of color dance across the sky.

An aurora happens when the sun makes something called *solar wind*. When the solar wind moves away from the sun, it carries with it tiny specks. These specks are called protons and electrons and are like electricity. The electrons and protons travel through space until they bump into the Earth's atmosphere. When this happens, the protons and electrons hit different particles in the atmosphere and discharge energy, which shows up in many different shapes and colors: red, blue, green, and violet.

An aurora occurs at the North Pole and the South Pole. When it appears above the North Pole, it is known as the *aurora borealis*, or northern lights. When it appears above the South Pole, it is known as the *aurora australis*, or southern lights. The aurora doesn't happen all the time. It only happens when the conditions are just right.

The best time to see an aurora is in winter and at night.